The world's greatest stunt duo is back – Great
Stupendo and his daughter, Little Stupendo!

Jon Blake started writing for children during his brief
career as a teacher. Since then he has had a number
of jobs, from community centre warden to part-time
lecturer. He is the author of several books for young
people, including *The King of Rock and Roll* and *The
Hell Hound of Hooley Street*, as well as the picture
books *Impo* and *You're a Hero, Daley B!* He
has written two other books about the famous
Stupendos: *Little Stupendo*, which was shortlisted for
the Children's Book Award, and *Little Stupendo Rides
Again*. He has also written plays for television and
the stage.

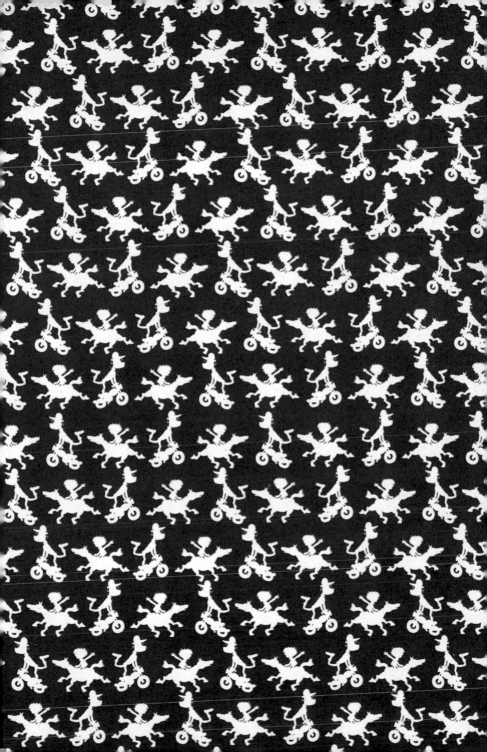

Books by the same author

Little Stupendo

Little Stupendo Flies High

The Supreme Dream Machine

JON BLAKE

Illustrations by Martin Chatterton

WALKER
BOOKS

This is a work of fiction. Names, characters, places and incidents are either the product of the author's imagination or, if real, are used fictitiously. All statements, activities, stunts, descriptions, information and material of any other kind contained herein are included for entertainment purposes only and should not be relied on for accuracy or replicated as they may result in injury.

First published 1999 by
Walker Books Ltd, 87 Vauxhall Walk
London SE11 5HJ

This edition published 2002

2 4 6 8 10 9 7 5 3

Text © 1999 Jon Blake
Illustrations © 1999 Martin Chatterton

The right of Jon Blake to be identified as author of this work has been asserted by him in accordance with the Copyright, Designs and Patents Act 1988.

This book has been typeset in Garamond.

Printed in China

British Library Cataloguing in Publication Data
A catalogue record for this book
is available from the British Library.

ISBN 978-0-7445-9051-7

www.walkerbooks.co.uk

CONTENTS

CHAPTER ONE

It had been a great year for the Stupendos. Little Stupendo and her father, the Great Stupendo, had become the most famous stunt duo in the world. People never knew what to expect when the Stupendos were in town.

The Great Stupendo
had jumped
seventeen
garden sheds
in a rocket-car …

flown over
the North Pole
standing on
a plane …

and dived off
Blackpool Tower
into a plastic
swimming pool.

Little Stupendo
had jumped
twelve double
beds on her
motorbike …

swum in the
ocean with a
man-eating
shark …

and skied down
Everest, the
highest mountain
in the world.

Every time the Great Stupendo
made an entrance, everyone clapped.

But whenever Little Stupendo
appeared, they cheered so loudly
that some people thought there was
an earthquake.

Every time the Stupendos
finished a show, a small crowd of
people lined up for the Great
Stupendo's autograph.

But the line of people waiting
for Little Stupendo was so long that
it went right out of town and into
the next one.

Needless to say, the Great Stupendo was very fed up with this. But whenever he moaned, Little Stupendo reminded him of something.

"Never forget," she said, "I saved your life once."

The Stupendos ended the year with a mammoth world tour. But once that was over, life got rather boring. They just weren't cut out for gardening or flower-arranging or collecting stamps.

Then, one day, the Great
Stupendo saw an advertisement:

"That's just the job for me!" said the Great Stupendo.

"Just the job for *us*, you mean!" said Little Stupendo.

The Great Stupendo went slightly red. "Yes, of course," he said. "That's what I meant."

CHAPTER TWO

Next day, the Stupendos arrived at
BIG PIX STUDIOS. It was a huge,
exciting place full of people
building things, moving things and
throwing tantrums.

This is the place for me, thought
Little Stupendo.

The audition was as easy as pie
for the Stupendos. They had to ride
the Wall of Death, walk a tightrope
over a hungry lion and fall
downstairs fifty-three times. Before it
was even over, the other stunt artists
had gone home. The Stupendos
were just too good for them.

It was time to meet Bob
Nosebite, the director.

Bob Nosebite wore glasses like
mirrors and munched one packet
of crisps after another.

"You can call me Bob," he said.

"You can call me Great," replied
the Great Stupendo.

"When can you start?" asked Bob.

"Now!" said Little Stupendo.

The Great Stupendo wasn't so sure. "What exactly is this film about?" he asked.

Bob Nosebite blew up a crisp packet, then burst it with a loud ...

"That's what it's about!" he said. "Bangs! Crashes! Smashes! Big explosions! Oh yes, and two people fall in love."

The Great Stupendo stroked his chin thoughtfully. "Hmm," he said. "This film doesn't sound at all suitable for a young girl."

"It sounds perfect!" cried Little Stupendo.

"Besides," said the Great Stupendo, "Little Stupendo has an awful lot of homework to do."

"No, I haven't!" cried Little Stupendo.

But Bob Nosebite believed the Great Stupendo. "I can see you care about your daughter," he said, "so I shall leave her out of the picture."

CHAPTER THREE

For the next week, the Great
Stupendo practised his stunts for
the film. He used the chairs, the
sofa and the kitchen table. He even
jumped out of a window on to
Little Stupendo's bed.

Meanwhile, Little Stupendo
sulked. "It isn't fair," she said.

Little Stupendo's frown grew
deeper and deeper. She wouldn't
sleep. She wouldn't eat. She
wouldn't even ride her motorbike.

The Great Stupendo decided he
had better cheer her up.

"I've got you a surprise!"
he announced one day.

"What is it?"
mumbled Little
Stupendo.

"Come with me,"
said the Great
Stupendo, "and
I will show you!"

The two Stupendos rode out of town. Little Stupendo began to get excited. I wonder if it's a jet-ski? she thought to herself. Or a hang-glider?

But they weren't going towards the shops. Or the beach. They were going into the country.

Suddenly, the Great Stupendo stopped by a field. In the field was an old horse.

"There!" he said. "That's your surprise, Little Stupendo!"

Little Stupendo's face dropped.

"Her name is Golden Wonderful," the Great Stupendo went on. "She used to be a famous racehorse."

Little Stupendo gazed at the tired old horse and sighed. Then a look of determination came over her face.

"I will train you," she said, "if it's the last thing I do."

CHAPTER FOUR

Little Stupendo had never ridden a horse. But that didn't put her off. It's just like a motorbike, she thought, with legs instead of wheels.

Little Stupendo climbed up on Golden Wonderful. "Go!" she shouted.

Golden Wonderful munched another mouthful of grass, flicked a few flies with her tail, then strolled lazily over to an interesting patch of nettles.

"Hmm," said Little Stupendo. "I never have this problem with the motorbike."

Little Stupendo practised all the stunts she did on her bike.

She rode
Golden Wonderful
backwards,

forwards,

cowboy-style

and side-saddle.

She stood
on one leg …

one hand …

one elbow …

and on her head.

But no matter what she did, Golden
Wonderful went just as slowly.

"I know!" said Little Stupendo. "She's run out of fuel!"

Little Stupendo took Golden Wonderful to Way-out Allan's filling station and parked her by the petrol pump.

"Fill her up, please!" she said.

Way-out Allan came out of the shop, munching on a bag of Dorkin's Do-nuts. Way-out Allan was often confused and sometimes thought he saw aliens. But he'd never seen a horse at a petrol pump.

Fill her up, please!

"Fill her up with what?" he asked.

"I don't know," said Little Stupendo. "What kind of fuel do horses use?"

At that moment there was a yell from Way-out Allan. "My do-nut!" he cried.

Golden Wonderful had eaten it.

"That's it!" said Little Stupendo.
"Do-nuts!"

Little Stupendo bought a whole
bag. Golden Wonderful gobbled
them down, one after the other,
and didn't leave a single crumb.

Then Little Stupendo shook the
reins. Golden Wonderful clopped
back to the field, just as slowly as
she came.

CHAPTER FIVE

Day after day, Little Stupendo tried her hardest with Golden Wonderful. But nothing she did seemed to make any difference.

Little Stupendo was getting *very* frustrated.

Meanwhile, the Great Stupendo was having the time of his life. Every night he told Little Stupendo about the great film he was making.

"You should have seen me!" he said. Then he leapt about the house describing all the stunts he'd done –

tumbling off
the roof of a
burning building ...

 wrestling
with a
twenty-foot
crocodile ...

smashing
his bike through
a wall of make-
believe bricks.

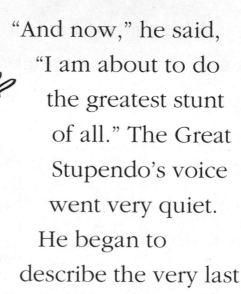

"And now," he said, "I am about to do the greatest stunt of all." The Great Stupendo's voice went very quiet. He began to describe the very last stunt in the film – one of the most dangerous stunts ever performed.

"I shall drive a car right on to the tracks of the railway," murmured the Great Stupendo. "The car will get stuck … the express train will come storming round the bend … and then, at the *very last* second, I shall leap out of the way!"

With that, the Great Stupendo
dived full-length on to the sofa and
sent the cat running for shelter.

Little Stupendo ground her teeth
in frustration. *I* want to do a great
stunt, she thought to herself.

CHAPTER SIX

Next day, Little Stupendo was more
determined than ever. She looked
at the stream that ran across the
field, then turned to Golden
Wonderful.

"We're going to jump that!" she
said.

But Golden Wonderful wasn't
interested in the stream. Golden
Wonderful was only interested in

the do-nut in Little Stupendo's hand.

Suddenly Little Stupendo had an idea.

If I fling this do-nut across the stream, she thought, Golden Wonderful will *have* to jump it!

Little Stupendo threw the do-nut with all her might. It landed perfectly on the other side of the stream. Golden Wonderful watched it and her mouth watered.

"Come on, girl!" cried Little Stupendo.

Golden Wonderful began to walk towards the stream.

"That's it, girl!" cried Little Stupendo. "We've got to jump the stream!"

But Golden Wonderful had no intention of jumping the stream. Golden Wonderful kept right on walking, straight down the bank, right into the freezing cold water. By the time they reached the other side, Little Stupendo was drenched to the skin.

Little Stupendo was
furious. She shook
her fist at Golden
Wonderful. "You…"
she cried. "You …
you … *stupid animal!*"

But the moment she said it, Little
Stupendo felt very, very sorry.
Golden Wonderful wasn't stupid.
She was old, that was all. She was
tired. Besides, she had never asked
to be a stunt horse.

"I know you're a nice old horse
really," said Little Stupendo, and
patted her nose, and imagined her
romping home in the Derby, many
years ago.

From now on, thought Little Stupendo, I'll stick to my motorbike.

But she was very sad to think this because, for the first time ever, she had failed.

With a heavy heart, Little Stupendo said goodbye to Golden Wonderful and tramped back to the gate.

Parked in the lane, as usual, was her motorbike.

Hmmm, thought Little Stupendo, at least I could jump the stream on this.

RRRRRRRRRM! Little Stupendo set off across the field, bumping and bouncing, eyes fixed on the stream ahead.

Suddenly, when she was half-way across the field, a white something-or-other flashed past.

Golden Wonderful!

Little Stupendo had never seen anything move so fast.

Little Stupendo screeched to a halt. Golden Wonderful reared up on her hind legs and neighed for all she was worth.

"*That's* what you needed!" cried Little Stupendo. "Something to race!"

Little Stupendo leapt up on to Golden Wonderful's back. The horse was full of life and itching to run. "After them!" cried Little Stupendo, pointing to the cars out on the road. Golden Wonderful was off like a shot. In one bound they cleared the fence, then galloped off down the road in a cloud of dust.

I'll show the Great Stupendo!
thought Little Stupendo.

The two raced on, right through
town, past BIG PIX STUDIOS and
up the hill which looked over the
railway line.

Down in the valley, the Great
Stupendo was getting ready for his
great stunt.

"Action!" cried Bob Nosebite.

The Great Stupendo revved up his car, smashed through a make-believe window, screamed round a corner on two wheels and raced for the railway line.

SCREEEECH! went the brakes.

CRASH! went the crossing barrier.

"Brilliant!" went
Bob Nosebite.

Just as planned,
the Great Stupendo
got stuck on the train
track. Just as planned, he watched
and waited for the train.

There was only one problem.

The Great Stupendo was looking
the wrong way.

"Dad!" shouted Little Stupendo from the hilltop. "Dad! you're looking the wrong way!"

But the Great Stupendo heard nothing. Meanwhile, the mighty train sped closer and closer.

There was only one thing for it.
With a shake of the reins, Little
Stupendo spurred Golden Wonderful
into action. "Race that train!" she
cried. They galloped into the valley
and after the train.

Golden Wonderful had never been so magnificent. Her hooves thundered and her nostrils flared. Soon they were alongside the train. Inch by inch they gained ground on it. At last they reached the front.

With an incredible leap, Little
Stupendo threw herself into the
driver's cab and with one last
desperate lunge, pulled hard on
the whistle.

The Great Stupendo turned. His jaw dropped. He jumped for his life. Next second the car was nothing but scrap metal.

When the train finally came to a halt, Little Stupendo climbed calmly down from the cab. There was a huge cheer.

"Brilliant!" cried Bob Nosebite.
"I must have that scene in the film!"
Little Stupendo smiled a big,
satisfied smile. "OK, Dad?" she said.

The Great Stupendo couldn't say no. After all, Little Stupendo had just saved his life … again!

Not long after, the posters were everywhere:

Yes, it really had been a great year
for Little Stupendo.